PUFFIN BOOKS

Allie's Crocodile

Angie Sage lives in Bristol and has two daughters aged twelve and seventeen. She studied illustration at Leicester Polytechnic and since then has illustrated many children's books. She started writing eight years ago and now writes and illustrates for ages three to ten. When Angie Sage is not writing or drawing, she likes walking along a Cornish beach and watching the sea.

Angie Sage

Allie's Crocodile

PUFFIN BOOKS

With thanks to Ben Baker
at Bristol Zoo

PUFFIN BOOKS

Published by the Penguin Group
Penguin Books Ltd, 27 Wrights Lane, London W8 5TZ, England
Penguin Books USA Inc., 375 Hudson Street, New York, New York 10014, USA
Penguin Books Australia Ltd, Ringwood, Victoria, Australia
Penguin Books Canada Ltd, 10 Alcorn Avenue, Toronto, Ontario, Canada M4V 3B2
Penguin Books (NZ) Ltd, 182–190 Wairau Road, Auckland 10, New Zealand

Penguin Books Ltd, Registered Offices: Harmondsworth, Middlesex, England

First published 1997
4

The moral right of the author/illustrator has been asserted

Filmset in Baskerville MT

Made and printed in England by Clays Ltd, St Ives plc

British Library Cataloguing in Publication Data
A CIP catalogue record for this book is available from the British Library

ISBN 0–140–38608–4

Chapter 1

"Excuse me," said the traffic warden, "you can't leave this crocodile here. This crocodile is illegally parked."

Allie looked up. She was trying to unlock her bike from the parking meter outside the carpet shop. It was raining and she couldn't remember the last number on her combination lock.

"What?" she said crossly.

"This meter bay is suspended," declared the traffic warden. "That means no parking. Not even crocodiles."

Allie looked down and saw a

greenish-brown crocodile lying in the parking bay. "It's not my crocodile," she said as she clicked in number seven. The lock opened.

"That's what they all say," said the traffic warden. "Not my car, not my crocodile. I've heard it all before."

"Well, it's not my crocodile," said Allie firmly as she put on her cycle helmet.

"In that case, miss, you'll have no objection if I arrange for it to be towed away." The traffic warden got out his radio.

Allie paused and looked down at the crocodile. "You *can't* tow it away," she objected.

"Ah-ha! So it *is* your crocodile." The traffic warden looked triumphant.

"I didn't say that," said Allie.

"Well, you can take it away now and we'll say no more about it, or you can

collect it from the pound and it will cost you one hundred and fifty pounds."

The crocodile stretched its short, stumpy legs and walked over to Allie. Allie was getting very wet and wanted to go home. "Oh, come on then," she said. She pushed her bike along the pavement, closely followed by the crocodile.

The traffic warden smugly folded his arms and watched them disappear as he waited for the next meter to run out.

Chapter 2

THE RAIN WAS still pouring down when
Allie and the crocodile arrived home.
Allie squelched into the garage and put
her bike away. The crocodile waddled
in after her. It left crocodile-shaped
footprints on the concrete floor.

"What am I going to do with a
soaking wet crocodile?" muttered Allie
to herself. "Oh *bother*!"

A gruff voice came from down by her
feet. "Thanks. Very kind, I'm sure.
When I was a short crocodile I was
taught manners. Taught to make my
guests feel welcome. Taught not to

moan about them when they were in my part of the river." The crocodile sniffed and stomped off towards the front door. "I hope your mother has better manners," it said.

Allie stood for a moment in the pouring rain. She opened her mouth as if to say something and then closed it again as the crocodile slid into the porch.

"Wait!" Allie yelled and ran after it. She tried to imagine what her mum would say about wet crocodile footprints in the hall. She couldn't even imagine what her mum would say about nice dry crocodile footprints.

The crocodile waited patiently in the porch. "Why," it asked slowly as if it was talking to someone very stupid, "why did you bring me home if you're not going to ask me in? Do you always leave people waiting outside?"

"Not *people* . . ." said Allie.

"Just crocodiles?"

"Yes – no. Oh, hang on a minute." Allie opened the door slowly and called out warily, "Mum?" There was no reply.

Then her brother shouted from his room, "Gone out. Back soon. Said get your own tea."

Allie stood back and let the crocodile slip into the hall. "Can you get up the stairs?" she asked. "You had better come and sit in my room."

The crocodile stomped slowly up the stairs. Allie opened her bedroom door and the crocodile slid in and lay on the floor. Allie noticed that it was covered with fluff from the carpet and looked very dry and dusty. The crocodile gazed around Allie's bedroom and blinked a little. "Where's your pond, then?" it asked.

"I haven't got a pond," said Allie.

"Not got a pond?"

"No . . . sorry."

The crocodile looked disappointed. It peered up at the bedroom ceiling. "Do you let the rain in, then? Sort of slide back the roof or something?" it asked hopefully.

"Er, no. Sorry. Look, I'll go and get you a drink. Would you like anything to eat?" Allie asked, hoping that it wouldn't.

"Water and fish, please," said the crocodile.

When Allie came back to her room with a bucket of water and some sardines, the crocodile had gone. She sat down on her bed with a sigh of relief. While she had been in the kitchen trying to open the tin of sardines, she had begun to realize just how complicated it was going to be having a crocodile to look after. Then she heard the sound of Mum's key in the front door.

"I'm ba-ack!" Mum called out.

"Hi, Mum!" Allie shouted happily. Then an awful thought struck her: how had the crocodile got out of the house? Suppose it hadn't? Suppose it was wandering around? Suppose it *ate Mum*?

"Eek!" Allie sprang to her feet just as the door to her bedroom opened.

It was her brother. "I'd get that crocodile out of the bath before Mum sees it; she'd have a fit. It's a good one. Really realistic. Did you get it at the joke shop?" He wandered off, chuckling to himself.

Chapter 3

ALLIE WOKE UP the next morning and sleepily stuck her foot out of bed. It landed on something cold and bumpy. It was then that she remembered the crocodile.

"Oh no . . ." she groaned and stuck her head under the pillow.

"Good morning. Is it raining?" the crocodile asked hopefully. It stretched its tail and yawned. A strong smell of fish filled Allie's bedroom.

"Oh pooh! Have you *ever* cleaned your teeth?" asked Allie.

"My teeth stay clean on their own.

You won't catch *me* putting a little pink brush with silly pictures on it in *my* mouth," sniffed the crocodile, who had watched Allie clean her teeth the night before while he had another quick soak in the bath.

The crocodile stretched lazily. "I'll just go and sit in that bath thing again," it said. It shuffled around until it was pointing in the direction of Allie's bedroom door and then started moving slowly.

Allie got to the door first and leaned against it. She took a deep breath and said, "Look, I'm sorry, but I'm not meant to have crocodiles in the house. I only took you home because the traffic warden was going to tow you away. This isn't a good place for you to stay. If Mum saw you she'd go mad."

The crocodile looked hurt. "Don't want to stay," it said grumpily. "Nasty dry place, this."

"Well . . . that's all right then," said Allie.

"Yes. That's all right then. I know when I'm not wanted," said the crocodile. It pushed past Allie and headed for the stairs. The next thing Allie heard was a thumpety-thump sound as the crocodile shot down the stairs and landed in a heap on the door mat.

"Allie! Are you all right?" shouted Mum from the bathroom.

Allie rushed down to the crocodile. "Fine! I'm fine, Mum!" she yelled. Mum came out of the bathroom and peered over the top of the stairs. Luckily she hadn't put her contact lenses in yet. All she saw was a greeny-brown bundle lying on the door mat.

"*Allie*, what on earth are you doing lying on the mat in your school raincoat on a Saturday?" she asked in a trying-to-be-patient voice.

"Oh, nothing, Mum," said Allie. "Just, um, you know . . . playing a game."

"Well, you could try playing at getting some breakfast instead." Mum stumbled back to the bathroom and put in her contact lenses. There was another shout. "Eurgh! Look at the state of this bath!"

Allie sat down by the crocodile. "Phew! That was close," she breathed. "Are you all right?"

16

The crocodile looked slightly shaken but it picked itself up. "Happens all the time. I'll be going then. Thanks for the fish."

Allie held open the front door and watched the crocodile waddle down the path. Somehow she didn't like seeing it go off on its own. "But it can't stay here," she told herself. "It needs to find someone who has a pond and a mum who likes crocodiles." Allie closed the door and went into the kitchen to get some cereal. There was no milk in the fridge.

Suddenly there was a loud yell from the front garden and the sound of breaking milk bottles. Allie ran to the window and saw the milkman speeding off in his milk float. Then she saw the crocodile heading towards the front gate. At that very moment, coming out of next door's front gate was Allie's neighbour, Ernest Python. Ernest

Python was the head keeper at the reptile house in the zoo. Allie knew she had to do something. Fast.

"Mum!" yelled Allie. "I'll just nip over to Gran's to borrow some milk!" She threw on her coat and ran out after the crocodile. She grabbed hold of its nose and tried to pull it under the hedge beside the gate.

"Oi!" the crocodile protested in a muffled voice.

Ernest Python, who was a nosy neighbour, loomed up and looked at Allie curiously.

"Hello, Mr Python," said Allie, trying to close the gate. There was something in the way.

"Good morning, Allie," replied Ernest Python, staring down at the gate. "That's an interesting crocodile tail you've got there," he said in a suspicious voice.

"It's great, isn't it? I got it yesterday. It's a sort of . . . joke thingy." Allie tried to shove the tail under the hedge with her foot. It was very heavy.

"Funny smell of fish around here," said Ernest Python. Allie did not answer; she wished he would go.

"Yes." Ernest Python smiled a reptile-like smile. "Thought I might have found a new crocodile for our happy little reptile house. Ha ha."

"Ha ha, Mr Python," said Allie politely. Ernest Python leaned forward and tried to peer over the gate. Allie slammed it shut on his foot.

"OUCH! Oh well . . . I must be getting off to work. There're crocodiles to feed and snakes to walk. Ha ha." He took one last look at the hedge and limped off down the street.

When Ernest Python was safely round the corner, Allie opened the gate.

"Come on," she said to the crocodile, "you're not safe on your own. Follow me. I've got an idea that might just work."

Allie set off down the street with the crocodile waddling after her.

Chapter 4

ALLIE AND THE crocodile arrived at a shiny red door. Allie rang the bell and waited.

"Hello, Gran," she said as the door opened slowly. "I've brought someone to see you."

"That's nice, Allie," said Gran, looking a little puzzled. "Who's that then, dear?"

Allie pointed down to the doorstep. "OH!" squeaked Gran. "Oh, my goodness me. It's a . . . OOH! Well I never!"

"It's a crocodile, Gran."

"Yes, dear, so it is. You had both better come inside."

"Thanks, Gran," said Allie as the crocodile slipped into Gran's house.

"Thanks, Gran," said the crocodile. "Most kind. Nice to meet someone with manners."

"Oh . . . goodness," gasped Gran. She went and sat down. "Allie dear, would you like something to eat? Have you had breakfast yet? It's very early. Perhaps your, er . . . friend would like something?"

"Water and fish, please, Gran," said the crocodile.

"Oh yes. Of course. Allie dear, I've got some tins of pilchards. They were little Tibbles' favourite. Poor Tibbles." Gran sniffed and looked for her hanky. Allie disappeared into the kitchen.

The crocodile coughed politely. "You have recently lost a loved one, Gran?"

he asked. "A much-loved crocodile?"

Gran blew her nose loudly. "Er, no. A cat. Tibbles was a cat."

Allie came back carrying a tray. On it was a cup of tea, a glass of milk, a plate piled high with pilchards and a bowl of water. She gave Gran her cup of tea and passed the water and fish to the crocodile.

"Thank you very much," said the crocodile.

"That's OK," said Allie. "Um . . . Gran . . ."

"Yes, dear?"

"Do you think . . . I mean, would you mind if . . . if the crocodile stayed with you for a while?"

Gran looked puzzled. "With me, dear?"

"Yes. He could stay in your pond. He misses his river and he can't stay with me cos Mum doesn't like dirty baths

and Mr Python lives next door and he might put him in a zoo and –"

"It's all right, Allie. Of course he can stay with me. He seems a very nice sort of crocodile."

The crocodile gulped down his last pilchard. "Wonderful fish, Gran," he said happily. "Now, if you could show me the way to your delightful pond, perhaps I could have my early morning soak."

Gran got up and led the way out to the pond. Allie drank her milk and watched them through the window. She saw Gran and the crocodile wandering down the garden path. Gran was showing the crocodile her best roses and her favourite apple tree, then she pointed towards the pond and the crocodile suddenly picked up speed across the lawn and slid gently into the water. He sank slowly down until Allie

could only see the tip of his nose and his two crocodile eyes peering out.

"Well, Allie," said Gran as she came back in, "I thought you said I should get another cat, not a *crocodile*. Still, it makes a nice change. I wonder if I should put in a bigger cat-flap?"

Chapter 5

ALLIE SKIPPED HOME past the letter-box, where she posted one of Gran's competition entries. Going in for competitions was Gran's hobby. The last thing she had won was a plastic seagull which lit up and sang the birdie song.

Allie was in the kitchen, putting the carton of milk that Gran had given her into the fridge, when her mum appeared. "Oh good, Allie, you've got some milk. There's broken bottles and milk all over the path. If you ask me, that Ernest Python has something to do with it. I've just caught him ferreting around under the hedge by the gate."

"Have some cornflakes, Mum." Allie did not want to talk about Ernest Python or broken milk bottles.

"Allie!" her brother burst into the kitchen. "Can I borrow your crocodile?"

"Don't be silly, Alan," said Mum. "Sit down and have some breakfast."

Allie gave her brother a kick. "Shut up about crocodiles, will you?" she hissed.

"Oh, excuse me for speaking," said Alan. "You can keep your silly crocodile to yourself then. I'll borrow Pete's dinosaur." He got up from the table. "It's inflatables day at the pool today, Mum. I'm off now. Want to get there early."

"That's nice, dear. What are you doing today, Allie?" asked Mum.

"Going to the pool with Emily." Allie

stuck her tongue out at Alan. "But we're not going near any silly boys. I'm going back to see Gran first. I want to see how the croc– um . . . how she is."

After breakfast Allie rushed back to Gran's. She let herself in through the side gate and went straight into the garden. The crocodile was in exactly the same place as he had been when she had left him. "How's the pond?" Allie asked him. The crocodile blew a few bubbles and sank down a little further.

Gran came out into the garden. "I think he's sleeping, Allie," she whispered. "He said he didn't get much sleep last night." Gran smiled a soppy smile. "He's lovely, isn't he?"

Allie grinned. "I knew you'd like him, Gran. Can he stay?"

"Of course he can, Allie. I'd be lonely without him. I'll feel much safer at

night knowing that there's a crocodile in my garden." Gran put her arm around Allie. "Now how about a nice glass of orange juice?"

"Sorry, Gran. I've got to meet Emily. We're going swimming."

The water in the pond suddenly bubbled up and the crocodile stuck his head out. "Swimming?" he asked. "I'll come with you."

"You can't," said Allie. "We're going to the swimming pool. It will be full of people. I can't take a crocodile into a swimming pool full of people."

"Why not?" asked the crocodile.

"Well . . ." Allie did not want to say anything that might hurt the crocodile's feelings.

"Because you think I'd eat them. That's it, isn't it?" The crocodile thumped his tail crossly and half the pond landed on Gran.

"Oooh!" she squeaked.

"Sorry, Gran," said the crocodile. He looked at Allie. "Well, I don't eat people. They taste *disgusting*. My great aunt ate one once and she was ill for days. Anyway, it would be very bad manners."

"But no one would let you into the pool," said Allie. "They don't allow crocodiles."

Gran looked at the crocodile

thoughtfully. "I hear it's inflatables day today," she said. "I'm sure if you didn't mind pretending to be an . . . er . . . a . . ." Gran stopped as she saw the crocodile's expression.

"Pretend to be one of those ridiculous plastic blow-up crocodiles?" he snapped.

"Er . . . yes," faltered Gran. "Not that you look anything like that of course. You are much, much better looking."

"All right then," said the crocodile.

Allie was amazed. "You mean you're going to be my inflatable for the day? That's great. I was going to have to share Emily's."

"Why not?" sighed the crocodile. "The things a crocodile has to do nowadays just to get a decent swim."

Chapter 6

GRAN WAVED GOODBYE as Allie and the crocodile walked happily down the street. The crocodile started to trot, and his scaly feet made a clicketty-clattery sound on the pavement.

"Slow down," Allie called out after him. "You're meant to be an inflatable, remember?"

"There's no need to be rude," snapped the crocodile.

Allie and the crocodile made their way to the swimming pool. Outside was a crowd of noisy people carrying all kinds of inflatables. Emily was waiting for Allie by the entrance. She was holding a huge pink elephant.

"Hi, you," grinned Emily. She looked at the crocodile and her eyes widened. "Hey, that's a brill inflatable. Where d'you get it?"

"Oh. Um, I got it in town. Yesterday. Let's go in, shall we?"

They bought their tickets and headed off to the changing rooms only to be stopped by the loud voice of an attendant.

"No inflatables in the changing rooms, please. Put them over there and pick them up when you're changed." The attendant pointed to a huge pile of blown-up ducks, submarines, hamburgers and hippos.

"What?" said Allie.

"Put that crocodile over there, please," said the attendant. "And that elephant."

The crocodile stared at the pile of coloured plastic. "He wants *me* to go *there*?"

"Yes," whispered Allie. "*Please*. We won't be long."

"*ME* . . . in a pile of plastic rubbish? You must be joking."

Emily had already dumped her elephant on to the pile. "Come on, Allie," she yelled as she disappeared into the changing rooms.

Allie got tough with the crocodile. "Look," she hissed, "either you get in that pile or you don't go swimming. It's up to you."

The crocodile shuffled off and sat between a dinosaur and a banana. He looked . . . well . . . snappy, thought Allie as she raced off after Emily.

Allie had never put on her swimming costume so quickly. She dashed out and collected the crocodile.

"What happened to that dinosaur –
and that banana?" she asked him. They
looked suspiciously flat.

"My teeth slipped. Can we *swim*
now?"

Allie decided that the sooner the
crocodile was in the pool the better.
They paddled through the footbath –
"Eurgh!" complained the crocodile as
the water went up his nose – and then
Allie jumped straight in. As she
surfaced, the crocodile slipped into the
water with a graceful swoop. He curved
down to the bottom of the pool and
then came up beside her.

"Wonderful. Deep water. Mmmm . . .
tastes funny. Tastes of humans and . . . ?"

"Chlorine," explained Allie.

"Ah," mumbled the crocodile. "I
prefer fish myself."

It was great for a while. Emily and
Allie splashed around and fell off

Emily's elephant while the crocodile swam quietly beneath them.

"You'll lose your crocodile if you're not careful," said Emily. "You ought to keep hold of it. Those boys are after it – look."

Allie looked. It was her brother and his horrible friends. Bother!

Her brother swam up. "Lend us your crocodile. Pete's dinosaur's got these massive holes in it. So has Greg's banana."

"No," said Allie. "Go away."

Her brother's friends splashed around. There were lots of them. They circled around Allie and Emily like a group of hungry sharks.

"Give it to me, Allie. It's not fair. We haven't got any inflatables and you girlies have got one each."

"Don't call me a girlie. Go away, Alan." Allie splashed him.

Suddenly one of the boys grabbed Emily's elephant. "OI!" yelled Emily,

and plunged after it. Alan grabbed
Allie to stop her helping Emily and the
boys piled on to the elephant. It began
to sink . . . and then, *whoosh*, it was
flying. Emily's elephant shot up into the
air and the boys tumbled off to find
themselves staring into the open jaws of
a crocodile. SNAP! went the crocodile.
SNAP, SNAP, SNAP!

"Help!" yelled Alan.

A loud whistle blew and the lifeguard ran over. "You!" he yelled at Allie. "You with the unhygienic inflatable – OUT!"

"But it was their fault," protested Allie, looking around for the boys. They were nowhere to be seen. There was only Alan who had gone a strange greenish colour and was hanging on to the side of the pool. Then Allie remembered the snapping sounds. "You didn't . . . you *haven't* . . . ?" she whispered to the crocodile.

"OUT!" said the lifeguard. He blew his whistle again. The crocodile swam to the steps at the shallow end and Allie followed him. They slowly got out of the pool.

"No, I did not," muttered the crocodile. "I told you, I don't eat humans. They're over there – look."

Allie looked and saw a shaky huddle of boys in the corner of the shallow end. "I bet they never knew they could swim so fast," she giggled.

Later, on the way home, the crocodile said, "I don't suppose we'll be going back to the swimming pool, will we?"

"No," said Allie, "I don't suppose we will."

"Humph," grunted the crocodile. "Where am I going to get a decent swim then?"

Chapter 7

IT WAS A cross crocodile that arrived
back at Gran's house with Allie. "I'm
going to my pond," he said. "I do not
wish to be disturbed."

Allie watched the crocodile slip off to
the back garden, then she let herself
into Gran's house.

"Allie, is that you?" Gran's voice
sounded strangely muffled.

"Where are you, Gran?" Allie called.

"In here, dear. I'm a bit stuck . . ."

Allie went into the sitting room. A
large yellow duck was sitting on the
sofa. "*Gran?*" gasped Allie.

"Thank goodness you're back, Allie," said the duck. "I can't get my head off."

Allie grabbed hold of the huge yellow fluffy head and pulled hard. It flew off with a *pop!* and Allie tumbled back on to the carpet.

"Gran, what *are* you doing?" asked Allie.

"Marjorie phoned, dear. Asked me to a fancy dress party tonight. Well, I told her I didn't want to go, but you know what Marjorie is like. Won't take no for an answer. So I went down to the fancy-dress-hire place and this was the only thing they had left." Gran sat on the edge of the sofa, her flushed face peeping out of the fluffy yellow costume.

"You look lovely, Gran," said Allie.

"No, I don't. I look daft. I can't go out on my own looking like this."

"But no one will know it's you," said Allie.

"*I* know it's me," said Gran. "I'm not going."

Allie helped Gran out of the duck suit. It was ages since Gran had been out and had fun, thought Allie. Ever since that terrible morning when Tibbles had fallen into the dust cart, Gran had stayed at home feeling sad. Allie had an idea, but first she needed to talk to the crocodile.

Gran was getting some fish out of the freezer when the crocodile pattered into the kitchen. "Hello, dear," smiled Gran. "It's hake today. That all right?"

"Lovely, thank you, Gran," said the crocodile. "My favourite, in fact."

"I thought cod was your favourite, dear," said Gran, putting six large fish into a bowl of cold water.

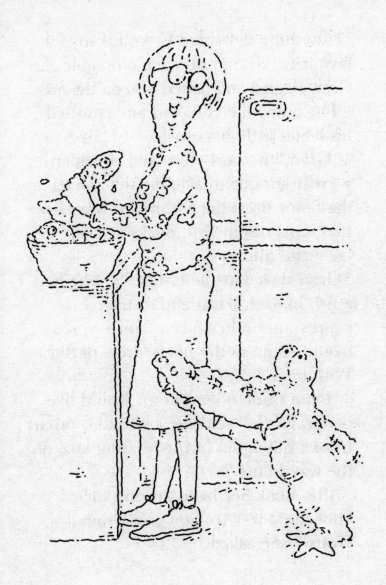

"Anything defrosted by you is my favourite, Gran," said the crocodile. Gran giggled and patted him on the nose.

The crocodile coughed and shuffled his feet a little nervously.

"Gran," he said, "I would consider it a great honour to accompany you to the fancy dress party tonight. May I say that, apart from fish, ducks are my favourite things."

Gran stared at the crocodile. She had a fish in each hand and a strange expression on her face. "You – you'd like to come to the fancy dress party? With me?"

"I can think of nothing I would like better, Gran," said the crocodile, "apart from a quick dip in the boating lake on the way home."

Allie stuck her head around the kitchen door. "Are you going then, Gran?" she asked.

Gran grinned. "Well, I don't think I've ever been asked out by a crocodile before. I'd love to go. Thank you."

The crocodile thumped his tail and looked pleased.

"But what are you going to dress up as?" Gran asked him.

"That's easy," laughed Allie. "A crocodile!"

"I'll have a bow tie, thank you," said the crocodile. "One must make an effort, don't you think?"

"Quite right," said Gran. "I'll go and sort out that duck suit right now."

Chapter 8

IT WAS GETTING dark when three
strange figures slipped out of Gran's
front gate. The smallest one walked
between the two large lumpy ones. "I
feel silly, Gran," it said as it tried to
keep up with a big duck and a
crocodile.

"You look lovely, dear," said the duck.
"I'm so glad I came across my old
teapot costume. I won first prize in that
when I was in the Brownies, you know."

"Yes, I *know*, Gran," sighed the small
pink teapot.

The party was in full swing when they

arrived. The crocodile, who had decided to stand upright for the night, took Gran's arm and escorted her inside. They disappeared into the crowd and left Allie standing by the door.

"Oh great," muttered Allie. "A load of old people all dressed up in silly clothes. Lovely."

"Hi, one lump or two?" a voice laughed in her ear.

Allie turned her head (not an easy thing to do inside a teapot) and saw a small purple fairy grinning at her. "Emily! What are *you* doing here?"

"Same as you," said Emily. "I'm looking completely stupid. Who made you come like *that*?"

"Gran," shouted Allie above the noise of the music, which someone had just turned up. "What about you?"

"Mum," shouted Emily. "She's here

with her friends. Mrs Python. And Mr
Python. Silly old bat. Not Mum. I
mean Mrs Python. This was her idea.
What a NOISE!"

"WHAT?" yelled Allie.

Someone had just turned the music
up even louder and everyone in the
room seemed to be stepping back,
leaving a space in the middle. This was
not good news for a small teapot, which
got stuck between a huge gorilla, a
penguin and a horrible fat snake. Allie
could not move; she had to stand and
watch as two dancers took to the floor,
a duck and a crocodile. Everyone
clapped as the crocodile twirled the
duck around and around. There were
"oohs" and "aahs" as the music got
faster and the crocodile thumped his
tail in time with the beat while the
duck deftly skipped around him. No
one had ever seen anything like it

before. No one, that is, except for Ernest Python. Ernest Python had seen lots of crocodiles before.

"OI! That's a crocodile!" shouted the fat snake next to Allie. Allie jumped. The snake was Ernest Python. His voice was so loud it could be heard above the music. People laughed. "Well done, Ernest. Glad to see you've learnt something after all those years at the reptile house!" The fat snake pushed forward towards Gran and the crocodile. He pushed up his snake head so that his mean little eyes could see the crocodile more clearly. Then he poked the crocodile in the ribs. The crocodile swung round and stared at Ernest Python.

"You're a crocodile," declared Mr Python. Everyone burst out laughing. Ernest Python began to get agitated. "It IS!" he shouted. "THAT is a

REAL crocodile. It should be in a ZOO!"

Suddenly the music stopped and everything went quiet. All eyes were on Ernest Python and the crocodile.

The crocodile began to thump his tail. He looked cross.

"Take your head off then," shouted Ernest Python excitedly in his high, whiny voice. "Let's see who you are."

People at the party began to mumble. "Well, he's right, you know, it *does* look like a crocodile." "Look at that tail. It looks real enough to me." "D'you think it'll bite?"

Meanwhile, Allie had been desperately trying to get out of her teapot. She *had* to do something. Finally she pushed up the lid and wriggled out, leaving it behind her, stuck between the gorilla and the penguin. She dashed over to Gran and the crocodile.

"Gran," she yelled, "I'm going to be SICK!"

Gran knew at once that this was her chance to get the crocodile out of the room safely. She grabbed the crocodile in one hand and Allie in the other and said in a very loud voice, "Come on, Allie – you can be sick in the garden, dear." Allie, Gran and a reluctant crocodile fled down the garden path.

"I was enjoying that, Gran," complained the crocodile. "It's a shame to leave now; you're a lovely dancer."

"And Ernest Python is a nasty busybody," said Gran. "You'll end up in the zoo if he has his way."

The crocodile was very quiet after that.

Chapter 9

ALLIE SKIPPED ON ahead, down the road that led to the park and the boating lake. Gran and the crocodile walked slowly behind and it wasn't until they had reached the edge of the boating lake that the crocodile said something: "SWIM . . . WATER . . . FISH."

He got down on to his tummy and his short legs paddled him into the lake with a gentle *splash*. Allie and Gran watched the dim crocodile-shape disappear into the night as he dived down into the muddy water of the boating lake.

Allie and Gran sat quietly on a bench by some old canoes, listening to the strange sounds of the night.

Quack, quack, *quack*! A flurry of ducks skidded along the water and hurtled into the safety of the bushes. Then there was a loud SPLASH! and a dull thump as all the boats on the other side of the lake rocked and moved on the water. Allie was sure she heard the shrill cry of a small furry animal. "Gran," she whispered, "what's he *doing*?"

Gran wriggled about in her rather scratchy duck costume and managed to get the duck head off.

"Don't worry, dear," she said. "He's just enjoying his swim."

"*Swimming* in the boating lake is prohibited . . . er, madam," said a loud voice behind them.

"Aargh!" screamed Gran. "Who's that?"

"I am the park keeper, madam. Persons swimming in the boating lake are prohibited under Section Three C Subsection Two of the Municipal Parks by-laws." The park keeper stared disapprovingly at Gran in her fluffy duck costume.

Gran stood up, folded her yellow fluffy wings and stared back crossly at the park keeper. "There aren't any *persons* swimming in the boating lake," she said. But the park keeper did not hear her. He was too busy staring at the sleek, dark shape of the crocodile as he cut through the still water on his way back to Gran.

The park keeper gave a small, strangled squeak as the crocodile slid out on to the bank and waddled over to Gran as fast as he could. "Are you all right, Gran?" puffed the crocodile. "I thought I heard you scream."

"Weeoorgh . . ." moaned the park keeper. He jumped into a canoe and paddled away as fast as any park keeper has ever paddled across a boating lake.

Gran patted the crocodile on the nose. "I'm fine, thank you. Perhaps we

should go home now. Did you have a nice swim, dear?"

"Fair to middling, thank you, Gran. Very muddy and no fish. Plenty of ducks, though. Nice voles, too."

"You *didn't* –" said Allie accusingly.

"Come on now, Allie," said Gran. "If you don't ask about ducks and voles, I won't ask about teapots. Particularly a large pink one that someone has left somewhere. OK?"

"That's different," mumbled Allie.

"What did you say, dear?"

"Nothing, Gran."

Allie, Gran and the crocodile walked slowly home along the high street. Suddenly the crocodile stopped in front of the travel agent. He was staring at a poster. On the poster was a picture of a beautiful river, with crocodiles basking on its banks. The words on the poster said:

**FLY TO AFRICA,
HOME OF THE CROCODILE.**
Flights available. Enquire within.

Gran joined the crocodile as he gazed
at the poster. The crocodile sighed a
big sigh and said, "I want to go home,
Gran. I want to go back to my river."

Gran put her arm around the
crocodile. "I know," she said sadly.

"I don't want to leave you, Gran. I
love staying with you, but I've got to
have somewhere to swim. You
understand that, don't you?" The
crocodile sniffed a little. So did Gran.

"I understand, dear," she said. "We'll
get you a ticket tomorrow."

Chapter 10

ALLIE STAYED THE night at Gran's
house. When she woke up the next
morning in the little spare bedroom she
drew back the curtains and looked out
of the window. The crocodile was
dozing in the pond. Allie gazed at him,
watching him blow bubbles up to the
surface of the water, and watching his
tail slowly flick from side to side. "I
wish he didn't want to go home," she
thought sadly.

After breakfast, Allie helped Gran
wash up. "I thought we had better go
down to the travel agent," sighed Gran.

"We did promise to book a plane ticket for him."

Allie put the last plate away. "I know, Gran. I'll miss him, though."

"Not as much as I will," said Gran. "We had such fun last night; he's such a lovely dancer. And so charming, so polite. I feel really safe with him in the back garden." Gran sighed and shook her head. "But he can't stay here without somewhere proper to swim. Come on, Allie, let's go and buy him a ticket back to his river."

The poster was still in the travel agent's window.

"In we go, then," said Gran. She marched up to a rather nervous young man sitting behind a large computer. It was his first day at work.

"I want to book a flight to Africa, home of the crocodile, just like your poster in the window says," said Gran.

The young man looked relieved. This was something he knew how to do. "Fine," he said as he fiddled with the keyboard. "When are you planning to go?"

"Oh, it's not for *me*, it's for a crocodile. He wants to go home as soon as possible."

"The first flight we have is tomorrow . . . er, excuse me, *who* did

you say it was for?" The young man
went a little pink.

"A crocodile. Tomorrow would be
fine," said Gran. The pink young man
swallowed nervously.

"Er . . . Do you mind if I just make a
phone call?" he gulped.

"Of course not, dear," said Gran.

The young man's hand shook as he
tapped out the numbers on his phone.

"Is that the zoo? Could you put me through to the reptile house, please?" he said in a whisper.

Gran nudged Allie, who was gazing at pictures of sandy beaches, and pulled her over to listen to the phone call.

"Yes . . . yes, I see," the young man was saying. "What? Lasso its tail? Oh, I see . . . and its head . . . yes . . . you put its head into a sack . . . oh . . . tranquillized . . . yes, in a very small crate so it can't break out . . . yes, yes, I'll ask. Thank you for your help, Mr Python." The young man put the phone down.

"It will have to go by air freight," he said. "We'd be very happy to arrange the crate for you."

"The *crate*?" spluttered Gran.

"Yes. Does the crocodile have an identification microchip?" the young man asked.

"A *what*?" said Gran.

"No? Well, it will need one of those. The zoo will be able to inject that."

"Inject?" gasped Allie. "He's got to have an *injection*?"

"Yes. And a certificate because he – er – the crocodile is an endangered species."

"I'm not surprised," muttered Gran, "if you treat them like that."

"Pardon?" said the young man, who was very pink by now. He wondered if this was a strange test that his boss had set him. He didn't think it was a fair test, not crocodiles on his first day.

"W-well," he stammered, "w-we can make all the arrangements for you if you could just give me the name of the z-zoo where the crocodile is kept."

"He's not in a zoo," snapped Gran, "he's in my pond." The phone fell out of the young man's hand and clattered on to the floor. He wasn't pink any more, he was pale grey.

Allie tugged at Gran's jacket. "Come on, Gran," she said, "let's go."

Gran nodded and allowed Allie to pull her out of the travel agent as the young man slid on to the floor with a thump.

Gran and Allie walked home silently. Gran was the first one to speak. "Well, are you going to tell him or am I?" she said.

"Tell him what exactly, Gran?"

"Tell him that he has to have an injection, that they are going to lasso him and stuff a sack over his head, tell him that he has to go in a *crate* . . ."

"You can tell him, Gran," said Allie.

Chapter 11

THE CROCODILE WAS waiting for them
when they got back. He was lying
quietly on the front lawn with his eyes
slowly opening and closing. He had
been dreaming of his river, dreaming of
diving down into the cool dark shadows
of the water, of basking in the gently
flowing current. He was woken up with
a start by the clang of the garden gate
as Allie slammed it shut.

"Oh!" said Gran. "I didn't expect to
see you there."

"Ah . . . hello, Gran," yawned the
crocodile as he remembered where he

was. "Did you get my plane ticket?"

"Er, no," said Gran. "I . . . um . . . Allie, you tell him."

The crocodile looked up suspiciously. "Tell him what?" he asked.

No one said anything. The crocodile thumped his tail crossly. "Tell him *what*?"

"Yougottogoinacrate," said Allie all in a rush.

The crocodile blinked. "A . . . *CRATE*?" he said slowly.

"Yes," said Allie.

The crocodile thumped his tail again. "I am NOT going in a crate. I came over rolled up in a smelly old carpet and I am going back in a proper seat. I want to watch the film. I want my lunch on one of those plastic trays and my duty-free drinks and I want to go and see the pilot in the cockpit."

With that, the crocodile lifted his

tummy off the ground and stood up. "I am going to sit in my pond. Oh, Gran, there's a letter for you there. The postman dropped it when he ran away. I tried to tell him to leave the post with me but he just made this strange noise. Funny chap." The crocodile disappeared off into the back garden.

"Oh deary deary dear," muttered Gran as she picked up the letter. "What are we going to do?"

"How about a cup of tea, Gran?" said Allie.

Gran was reading the letter when Allie brought in the tea.

"Bother!" said Gran. "I haven't won the car. I've only won second prize."

Allie was excited. "You mean you've won a *prize*? What is it, Gran?"

"Don't go getting excited, dear. It's something boring to do with the

garden. Here, you have a look." Gran passed the letter over to Allie.

Allie read it out: "'Congratulations! You have WON second prize in the Name That Pilchard competition sponsored by Pook's Prime Pilchards. You have WON, courtesy of Pook's Prime Pilchards, a complete *new look* for your garden! But most exciting of all, you have WON *one hundred boxes* of our Brand New Prime Pilchard Jelly (a new concept in puddings).'"

"Wow, Gran, that's great!" said Allie.

"But I wanted the first prize. It was a lovely car," grumbled Gran, "and I don't know *where* we're going to put all those boxes of that disgusting Pilchard Jelly either. I've got enough to worry about with that poor crocodile."

Allie gazed out of the window at the crocodile in the pond. She wished Gran wasn't so worried about him. She

wished he had somewhere nice to swim
so that he could stay with Gran. She
wished the whole garden was a pond
big enough and deep enough for him to
live in. She wished . . . "Gran!"
shouted Allie.

"Ooh! What dear? You made me
jump," said Gran.

"Gran, *Gran*! I've got this great idea!"
Allie jumped up and dragged Gran
over to the window. "Look!" she said.

"Yes, dear, that lovely crocodile in his
tiny pond, and somehow we have to get
him home."

"No, we don't, Gran. He can stay
here now! With your prize we can make
the whole garden into the biggest pond
ever!"

Chapter 12

POOK'S PRIME PILCHARDS had never heard anything like it. "You want *what*, madam?" the Pilchard person spluttered at the other end of the phone.

"I want", repeated Gran, "my entire garden made into a lake. I want one large island and two small ones. I want underwater rocks and a small creek and – er, hang on a minute, please . . . what did you say, dear?" she whispered to the crocodile. "Oh yes, fish. Lots of fish. Got that?"

"But, madam," objected the Pilchard

person, "we were only expecting to plant a few shrubs, maybe dig up a few weeds. I suppose we could run to a gazebo. Can I tempt you with a gazebo, madam?"

"No," snapped Gran, "you can't. Now you get straight over here and start digging. Goodbye."

The Pilchard people got straight over and started digging. The crocodile moved into the bathroom and, although Allie ran him plenty of deep baths, he spent most of the time gazing out of the window, watching as his own lake began to take shape.

It was an exciting evening two weeks later when Pook's Pilchards drove their diggers away. Gran gazed at the muddy mess that had once been her garden.

"Well," she sighed, "it will all be worth it once I see that crocodile swimming around."

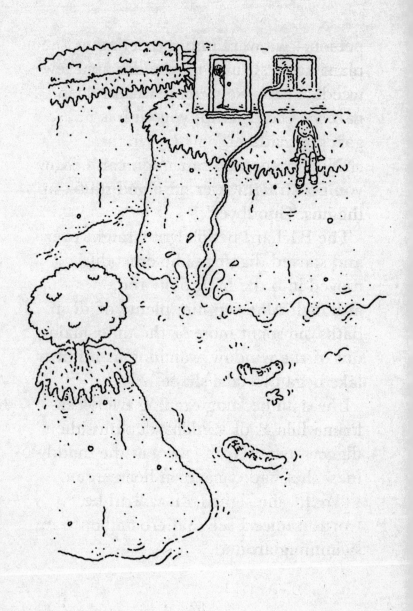

Allie clambered into the dry lake. She ran down to the deepest part in the middle and looked up. It was so deep that she could hardly see Gran's house.

"It's *great!*" she shouted up to the crocodile, who was peering over the edge.

"Good," said Gran. "I'll go and fix up the hose pipe."

The lake slowly filled up; slowly, slowly every day the water rose. The crocodile floated happily around in the shallows to begin with, then, as the days went on, he found that he could dive down and spin round and round, just as he had done in his river.

The day the lake was full, a Pook's Prime Pilchards van drew up outside Gran's house.

"One hundred boxes of Prime Pilchard Jelly," said the van driver, "and a tank of fish. Where do you want them, madam?"

"Out the back, please," said Gran.
Moments later there was a loud splash
and a scream. Gran rushed round to
find Allie pulling the van driver out of
the lake and shooing the crocodile
away.

"Sorry, Gran," mumbled the crocodile. "It must have been the smell of that jelly stuff. For a moment I thought he was a giant pilchard."

Gran dried out the van driver and sent him on his way.

That evening, Gran, Allie and the crocodile had a lake-warming party. Gran made a fish picnic and a huge plate of pilchard jelly. She also had a surprise for Allie.

"Ooh!" said Allie, when she saw the present wrapped up in fish wrapping paper. "What is it?"

"Open it and see," smiled Gran.

Allie opened it and pulled out a large piece of floppy blue and yellow plastic. "What *is* it, Gran?"

"It's a boat," laughed Gran, "a little dinghy. We'll blow it up and then you can explore the lake and row over to the big island."

Allie was thrilled. "Oh *thank you*, Gran!" She threw her arms around Gran and gave her a big hug.

"No," said Gran. "Thank *you*, dear, for bringing this lovely crocodile to stay with me."

Gran and Allie blew up the boat while the crocodile ate all the pilchard jelly. Then Gran sat happily on the side of her brand new lake and watched Allie and the crocodile chasing each other around the big island.

"Well," Gran said to herself, "this is much more fun than Tibbles ever was."